Agnes of God

A DRAMA

by John Pielmeier

SAMUEL FRENCH, INC.
45 WEST 25th STREET   NEW YORK 10010
7623 SUNSET BOULEVARD   HOLLYWOOD 90046
LONDON   *TORONTO*

Agnes of God was first presented in a staged reading at the 1979 Eugene O'Neill Playwrights Conference on July 26, 1979. It was directed by Robert Allan Ackerman, and the cast was as follows:

DOCTOR MARTHA LIVINGSTONE .... Jo Henderson
MOTHER MIRIAM RUTH .... Jacqueline Brookes
AGNES .... Dianne Wiest

The first professional production of *Agnes of God* opened on March 7, 1980 at the Actors Theatre of Louisville, Jon Jory Producing Director. It was directed by Walton Jones, with sets and lights by Paul Owen, and costumes by Kurt Wilhelm. The cast was as follows:

DOCTOR MARTHA LIVINGSTONE .... Adale O'Brien
MOTHER MIRIAM RUTH .... Anne Pitoniak
AGNES................................. Mia Dillon

Agnes of God opened on Broadway at the Music Box Theatre on March 30, 1982. It was presented by Kenneth Waissman, Lou Kramer, and Paramount Theatre Productions, and directed by Michael Lindsay-Hogg, with sets by Eugene Lee, lighting by Roger Morgan, and costumes by Carrie Robbins. The cast was as follows:

DOCTOR MARTHA LIVINGSTONE .... Elizabeth Ashley
MOTHER MIRIAM RUTH .... Geraldine Page
AGNES .... Amanda Plummer

THE CHARACTERS

DOCTOR MARTHA LIVINGSTONE pronounced "Li-ving-
stun")
MOTHER MIRIAM RUTH
AGNES

The play is best served, I believe, by a stage free of all
props, furniture and set pieces. The scenes flow one into
another, without pause. Characters appear and disap-
pear, and may even be present onstage when not in a
particular scene. Because it is a play of the mind, and
miracles, it is a play of light and shadows.

All parentheses in the dialogue indicate lines that are
cut off or overlapped before the parentheses begin.

Throughout the evening, the doctor is never without a
cigarette, except in her monologues and one or two
other moments indicated in the script, until the end of
the first act, after which she never smokes again.

— JOHN PIELMEIER

THE MUSIC

If possible, the music should be sung live by the actress
playing Agnes. Depending on the set and the interpreta-
tion, all characters may be visible onstage at all times.

Of the following tunes, "Virgin Mary," "Basiez Moy,"
and "Charlie's Neat" should be sung as written. The
others are suggestions for the Mass that Agnes sings;
more appropriate ones may be found. The music must
not be *too* familiar, and should never be slow or dolor-
ous: Agnes is at her most glorious when singing.

SAMUEL FRENCH, INC. can supply **amateurs** with
vocal music which is needed for the play upon receipt of
$3.00, plus $1.00 for postage and handling, plus a $7.50
per production music royalty. **Stock** terms quoted on
application.

To The Lady

"'. . . why do you worry? What good would it do you if I told you she is indeed a saint? I cannot make saints, nor can the Pope. We can only recognize saints when the plainest evidence shows them to be saintly. If you think her a saint, she is a saint to you. What more do you ask? That is what we call the reality of the soul; you are foolish to demand the agreement of the world as well. . . .'

"'But it is the miracles that concern me. What you say takes no account of the miracles.'

"'Oh, miracles! They happen everywhere. They are conditional. . . . Miracles are things that people cannot explain. . . . Miracles depend much on time, and place, and what we know and do not know. . . . Life is too great a miracle for us to make so much fuss about petty little reversals of what we pompously assume to be the natural order. . . . Who is she? That is what you must discover . . . and you must find your answer in psychological truth, not in objective truth. . . . And while you are searching, get on with your own life and accept the possibility that it may be purchased at the price of hers and that this may be God's plan for you and her.'"

ROBERTSON DAVIES,
Fifth Business

Agnes of God

ACT ONE

Scene 1

Darkness. A beautiful soprano voice is heard singing.

AGNES. *Kyrie eleison. Kyrie eleison. Kyrie eleison. Christe eleison. Christe eleison. Kyrie eleison.*

(The lights softly rise on DOCTOR MARTHA LIVINGSTONE.)

DOCTOR. I remember when I was a child I went to see Garbo's *Camille,* oh, at least five or six times. And each time I sincerely believed she would *not* die of consumption. I sat in the theater breathless with expectation and hope, and each time I was disappointed, and each time I promised to return, in search of a happy ending. Because I believed in the existence of an alternate last reel. Locked away in some forgotten vault in Hollywood, Greta Garbo survives consumption, oncoming trains, and firing squads. Every time. I still want to believe in alternate reels. I still want to believe that somewhere, somehow, there is a happy ending for *every* story. It all depends on how thoroughly you look for it. And how deeply you need it. (*silence*) The baby was discovered in a wastepaper basket with the umbilical cord knotted around its neck. The mother was found unconscious by

7

the door to her room, suffering from excessive loss of blood. She was indicted for manslaughter and brought to trial. Her case was assigned to me, Doctor Martha Livingstone, as court psychiatrist, to determine whether she was legally sane. I wanted to help . . . (this young woman, believe me.)

ACT ONE

SCENE 2

MOTHER. Doctor Livingstone, I presume? (*MOTHER laughs at her own joke.*) I'm Mother Miriam Ruth, in charge of the convent where Sister Agnes is living.

DOCTOR. How do you do.

MOTHER. You needn't call me Mother, if you don't wish.

DOCTOR. Thank you.

MOTHER. Most people find it uncomfortable.

DOCTOR. Well . . .

MOTHER. I'm afraid the word brings up the most unpleasant connotations in this day and age . . .

DOCTOR. Yes.

MOTHER. . . . or it forces a familiarity that most are not willing to accept, right off the bat.

DOCTOR. I see.

MOTHER. So you may call me Sister. I've brought Sister Agnes for her appointment. They're allowing her to stay at the convent until the trial.

DOCTOR. Yes, I . . . (know.)

MOTHER. And I wanted to offer my help.

DOCTOR. Well, thank you, Sister, but I haven't even *met* Sister Agnes yet. If there's anything unclear *after* I speak to her, I'd . . . (be happy to talk to you.)

MOTHER. You must have tons of questions.

DOCTOR. I do, but I'd like to ask them of Agnes.

MOTHER. She can't help you there.

DOCTOR. What do you mean?

MOTHER. She's blocked it out, forgotten it. I'm the only one who can answer those questions.

DOCTOR. How well do you know her?

MOTHER. Oh, I know Sister Agnes very well. You see, we're a contemplative order, not a teaching one. Our ranks are quite small. I was chosen to be Mother Superior about four years ago, just prior to her coming to us. So I think I'm more than qualified to answer any questions you might have. Would you mind not smoking?

DOCTOR. Yes, I'm sorry, I should have asked if it bothered you. (*The DOCTOR does not put out the cigarette, but waves the smoke in another direction.*)

MOTHER. Never offer an alcoholic a drink, isn't that what they say?

DOCTOR. You were a smoker?

MOTHER. Two packs a day.

DOCTOR. Oh, I can beat that, Sister.

MOTHER. Lucky Strikes. (*The DOCTOR laughs.*) My sister used to say that one of the few things to believe in in this crazy world is the honesty of unfiltered cigarette smokers.

DOCTOR. You have a smart sister.

MOTHER. And you have questions. Fire away. (*silence*)

DOCTOR. Who knew about Agnes' pregnancy?

MOTHER. No one.

DOCTOR. How did she hide it from the other nuns?

MOTHER. She undressed alone, she bathed alone.

DOCTOR. Is that normal?

MOTHER. Yes.

DOCTOR. How did she hide it during the day?

MOTHER. (*shaking her habit*) She could have hidden a machine gun in here if she wanted.

DOCTOR. And she had no physical examination during this time?

MOTHER. We're examined once a year. Her pregnancy fell in between our doctor's visits.

DOCTOR. Who found the baby?

MOTHER. I did. I'd given Sister Agnes permission to retire early that night. She wasn't feeling very well. I went to her room a short while later . . .

DOCTOR. The nuns have separate rooms?

MOTHER. Yes. And I found her unconscious by the door. I tried to revive her. When I couldn't I had one of the other sisters call for an ambulance. It was then that I found . . . the wastepaper basket.

DOCTOR. Found?

MOTHER. It was hidden. Against the wall, under the bed.

DOCTOR. Why did you think to look there?

MOTHER. I was cleaning. There was a lot of blood.

DOCTOR. Were you alone when you found it?

MOTHER. No. Another sister, Sister Margaret, was with me. It was she who called the police.

DOCTOR. Did you find a diary, letters?

MOTHER. I don't understand.

DOCTOR. Something to clue you in on the identity of the father.

MOTHER. Oh I see. No, I found nothing.

DOCTOR. Who could it have been?

MOTHER. I haven't a clue.

DOCTOR. What men had access to her?

MOTHER. None, as far as I know.

DOCTOR. Was there a doctor?

MOTHER. Yes.

DOCTOR. A man?

MOTHER. Yes, but I told you she never . . . (saw him.)

DOCTOR. Was there a priest?

MOTHER. Yes, but . . . (I don't see . . .)

DOCTOR. What's his name?

MOTHER. Father Marshall. But I don't see him as a candidate. He's very shy.

DOCTOR. Could there have been anyone else?

MOTHER. Obviously there was.

DOCTOR. Then why didn't you care to find out who?

MOTHER. Believe me, I cared very much at the time. I did everything short of asking Agnes, and still . . . (I have no idea how she got that child.)

DOCTOR. Why *didn't* you ask her?

MOTHER. If she doesn't even remember the birth, do you think she'd admit to the conception? Besides, I really don't see what this has to do with her.

DOCTOR. Oh, come on, Sister.

MOTHER. The *important* fact is that *somebody* gave her that baby, Doctor. That we know. But that happened some twelve months ago. I fail to see how the *identity* of that somebody has anything to do with the trial.

DOCTOR. Why do you think that?

MOTHER. Don't ask me those questions, dear. I'm not the patient.

DOCTOR. But *I'm* the doctor. *I'm* the one who decides what is or is not important here.

MOTHER. Yes.

DOCTOR. Then why are you avoiding my question?

MOTHER. I'm not . . . (avoiding.)

DOCTOR. Who was the father?

MOTHER. I don't know. (*silence*)

DOCTOR. I'd like to see her now.

MOTHER. Doctor, I don't know how to say this politely, but I don't approve of you. Not you personally, but —

DOCTOR. The science of psychiatry.

MOTHER. Yes. I want to ask you to deal with Agnes as speedily and as easily as possible. She's a fragile person. She won't hold up under *any* sort of cross-examination.

DOCTOR. Sister, I'm not with the Inquisition.

MOTHER. And I'm not from the Middle Ages. I know what you are. You're a surgeon. I don't want that mind cut open.

DOCTOR. Is there something in there you don't . . . (want me to see?)

MOTHER. I want you to be careful, that's all.

DOCTOR. And quick?

MOTHER. Yes.

DOCTOR. Why?

MOTHER. Because Agnes is different.

DOCTOR. From other nuns? Yes, I can see that.

MOTHER. From other people. She's special.

DOCTOR. In what way?

MOTHER. She's gifted. She's blessed.

DOCTOR. What do you mean? (*AGNES is heard singing.*)

AGNES. *Gloria in excelsis Deo . . .*

MOTHER. There.

AGNES. *Et in terra pax hominibus bonae voluntatis.*

MOTHER. She has the voice of an angel.

AGNES. *Laudamus te.*
Benedicimus te.

DOCTOR. Does she often sing when she's alone?

MOTHER. Always.

AGNES. *Adoramus te.*

MOTHER. She's embarrassed to sing in front of others.

AGNES. *Glorificamus te.*

DOCTOR. Who taught her?

MOTHER. I don't know.

AGNES. *Gratias agimus tibi propter magnam gloriam tuam.*
Domine Deus.
Rex coelestis.
Deus pater omnipotens.
Domini Fili unigenite
Jesu Christe.

MOTHER. (*during above*) When I first heard her sing, I was thrilled. And I couldn't connect that voice with the simple, happy child I knew. And she *was* happy, Doctor. But that voice belongs to someone else.

AGNES. *Domine Deus,*
Agnus Dei,
Filius Patris,
Qui tollis peccata mundi,
Miserere nobis.

DOCTOR. Would you send her in, please?

MOTHER. You will be careful, won't you?

DOCTOR. I'm always careful, Sister.

MOTHER. May I stay?

DOCTOR. No. (*MOTHER smiles.*)

MOTHER. I'll send her in.

ACT ONE

SCENE 3

AGNES continues to sing into this scene.

AGNES. *Qui tollis peccata mundi*
Suscipe deprecationem nostram,
Qui sedes ad dexteram Patris,
Miserere nobis.

Quoniam tu solus sanctus,
Tu solus Dominus,
Tu solus Altissimus,
Jesu Christe.
Cum Sancto Spiritu
In gloria Dei Patris.

DOCTOR. (*speaking over AGNES*) There was a lynching mob that came before a judge who accused them of hanging a man without a fair and objective trial. "Oh, your Honor," the leader said, "we listened *very* fairly and objectively to *every* word he had to say. Then we hung the son of a bitch." I *wanted* to maintain my objectivity, but Mother Miriam wouldn't believe that. Oh, she couldn't have known about Marie but she must have suspected *something*. Marie was my younger sister, who decided she had a vocation to the convent when she was fifteen. So my mother sent her off without a second thought, and I never saw her again. I received a message late one night that Marie had died of acute, and unattended, appendicitis because her Mother Superior wouldn't send her to a hospital. (*She laughs.*) Well, no, I guess at heart I couldn't be very fair and objective, could I? But I tried. (*silence*) I remember waiting to view Marie's body in a little convent room, and staring at those spotless walls and floors and thinking, my God, what a metaphor for their minds. And that's when I realized that *my* religion, *my* Christ, is this. The mind. Everything I do not understand in this world is contained in these few cubic inches. Within this shell of skin and bone and blood I have the secret to absolutely everything. I look at a tree and I think, isn't it wonderful that I have created something so *green*. God isn't out there. He's in here. God is you. Or rather you are God. Mother Miriam couldn't understand that, of course.

Oh, she reminded me so much of my own mother. And as for Agnes, well . . . (just hearing her voice . . .) (*The DOCTOR is interrupted by AGNES' appearance.*)

ACT ONE

Scene 4

AGNES. Hello.

DOCTOR. Hello. I'm Doctor Livingstone. I've been asked to talk to you. May I?

AGNES. Yes.

DOCTOR. You have a lovely voice.

AGNES. No I don't.

DOCTOR. I just heard you.

AGNES. That wasn't me.

DOCTOR. Was it my receptionist? You saw her, didn't you? The tall woman with the purple hair who looks like an ostrich? (*AGNES smiles.*) That's not very nice to say, but she does, doesn't she?

AGNES. Yes.

DOCTOR. She wasn't singing now, was she? I remember one day she sang and broke a patient's eyeglasses. (*AGNES laughs.*) You're very pretty, Agnes.

AGNES. No I'm not.

DOCTOR. Hasn't anyone ever told you that before?

AGNES. I don't know.

DOCTOR. Then I'm telling you now. You're very pretty. And you have a lovely voice.

AGNES. Let's talk about something else.

DOCTOR. What would you like to talk about?

AGNES. I don't know.

DOCTOR. Anything. First thing comes to your mind.

AGNES. God. But there's nothing to say about God.
DOCTOR. Second thing comes to your mind.
AGNES. Love.
DOCTOR. Why love?
AGNES. I don't know. (*silence*)
DOCTOR. Have *you* ever loved someone, Agnes?
AGNES. God.
DOCTOR. I mean have you ever loved another human?
AGNES. Oh, yes.
DOCTOR. Who is that?
AGNES. Everyone.
DOCTOR. Who in particular?
AGNES. Right now?
DOCTOR. Yes.
AGNES. I love you. (*silence*)
DOCTOR. But have you ever loved a man? Other than
Jesus Christ.
AGNES. Yes.
DOCTOR. Who?
AGNES. Oh, there are so many.
DOCTOR. Well, do you love Father Marshall?
AGNES. Oh, yes.
DOCTOR. Do you think *he* loves *you?*
AGNES. Oh, I know he does.
DOCTOR. He told you that?
AGNES. No, but when I look into his eyes I can see.
DOCTOR. You've been alone together.
AGNES. Oh, yes.
DOCTOR. Often?
AGNES. At least once a week.
DOCTOR. (*sharing AGNES' joy*) Did you like that?
AGNES. Oh, yes.
DOCTOR. Where do you meet?
AGNES. In the confessional. (*a beat*)

DOCTOR. I see. Do you ever meet with him . . . (outside the confessional?)

AGNES. You want to talk about the baby, don't you?

DOCTOR. Would you like to talk about it?

AGNES. I never saw any baby. I think they made it up.

DOCTOR. Who?

AGNES. The police.

DOCTOR. Why should they?

AGNES. I don't know.

DOCTOR. Do you remember the night they said it came?

AGNES. No. I was sick.

DOCTOR. How were you sick?

AGNES. Something I ate.

DOCTOR. Did it hurt?

AGNES. Yes.

DOCTOR. Where?

AGNES. Down there.

DOCTOR. What did you do?

AGNES. I went to my room.

DOCTOR. What happened there?

AGNES. I got sicker.

DOCTOR. And then?

AGNES. I fell asleep.

DOCTOR. In the middle of all that pain?

AGNES. Yes.

DOCTOR. But where did the baby come from?

AGNES. What baby?

DOCTOR. The baby they made up.

AGNES. From their heads.

DOCTOR. Is that where they say it came from?

AGNES. No, they say it came from the wastepaper basket.

DOCTOR. Where did it come from before that?

AGNES. From God.

DOCTOR. *After* God, *before* the wastepaper basket.

AGNES. I don't understand.

DOCTOR. How are babies born?

AGNES. Don't you know?

DOCTOR. Yes, I think I do, but I want you to . . . (tell me.)

AGNES. I don't know what you're talking about! You want to talk about the baby, everybody wants to talk about the baby, but I never saw the baby, so I can't talk about the baby, because I don't believe in the baby!

DOCTOR. Then let's talk about something else.

AGNES. No! I'm tired of talking! I've been talking for weeks! And nobody believes me when I tell them anything! Nobody listens to *me!*

DOCTOR. I'll listen. That's my job.

AGNES. But I don't want to have to answer any more questions.

DOCTOR. Then how would you like to ask them?

AGNES. What do you mean?

DOCTOR. Just like that. You ask, I'll answer.

AGNES. Anything?

DOCTOR. Anything. (*a beat*)

AGNES. What's your real name?

DOCTOR. Martha Louise Livingstone.

AGNES. Are you married?

DOCTOR. No.

AGNES. Would you like to be?

DOCTOR. Not at the moment, no.

AGNES. Do you have children?

DOCTOR. No.

AGNES. Would you like some?

DOCTOR. I can't have them anymore.

AGNES. Why?

DOCTOR. Well . . . I stopped menstruating.

AGNES. Why do you smoke?

DOCTOR. Does it bother you?

AGNES. No questions.

DOCTOR. Smoking is an obsession with me. I started smoking when my mother died. She was an obsession, too. I suppose I'll stop smoking when I become obsessed with something else. (*silence*) I bet you're sorry you asked. Any more questions?

AGNES. One.

DOCTOR. What's that?

AGNES. Where do *you* think babies come from?

DOCTOR. From their mothers and fathers, of course. Before that, I don't know.

AGNES. Well, I think they come from when an angel lights on their mother's chest and whispers into her ear. That makes good babies start to grow. Bad babies come from when a fallen angel squeezes in down there, and they grow and grow until they come out down there. I don't know where good babies come out. (*silence*) And you can't tell the difference except that bad babies cry a lot and make their fathers go away and their mothers get very ill and die sometimes. Mummy wasn't very happy when *she* died and I think she went to hell because everytime I see her she looks like she just stepped out of a hot shower. And I'm never sure if it's her or the Lady who tells me things. They fight over me all the time. The Lady I saw when I was ten. I was lying on the grass looking at the sun and the sun became a cloud and the cloud became the Lady, and she told me she would talk to me and then her feet began to bleed and I saw there were holes in her hands and in her side and I tried to catch the blood as it fell from the sky but I couldn't see any more because my eyes hurt because there were big black spots in front of them. And she tells me things like—right now she's crying "Marie! Marie!" but I don't know what that means. And she uses me to sing. It's as if she's throwing a big hook through the air and it catches me under my ribs and tries to pull me up but I can't move because Mummy is holding my feet and all I can do is sing in her voice, it's the Lady's voice, God loves you! (*silence*) God loves you. (*silence*)

DOCTOR. Do you know a Marie?

AGNES. No. Do you? (*silence*)

DOCTOR. Why should I?

AGNES. I don't know. (*silence*)

DOCTOR. Do you hear them often, (these voices?)

AGNES. I don't want to talk anymore, all right? I just want to go home.

ACT ONE

SCENE 5

MOTHER. Well, what do you think? Is she totally bananas or merely slightly off center? Or maybe she's perfectly sane and just a very good liar. What have you decided?

DOCTOR. I haven't yet. What about you?

MOTHER. Me?

DOCTOR. Yes. You know her better than I do. What's your opinion?

MOTHER. Well . . . I believe that she's . . . *not* crazy. Nor is she lying.

DOCTOR. But how could she have a child and know nothing of sex and birth?

MOTHER. Because she's an innocent. She's a slate that hasn't been touched, except by God. There's no place for those facts in her mind.

DOCTOR. Oh, bullshit.

MOTHER. In her case it isn't. Her mother kept her home almost all of the time. She's had very little schooling. I don't know how her mother avoided the authorities but she did. When her mother died, Agnes came to us. She's never been "out there," Doctor. She's never seen a television show or a movie. She's never read a book.

DOCTOR. But if you believe she's so innocent, how could she murder a child?

MOTHER. She didn't. This is manslaughter, not murder. She did not consciously kill that baby. I don't know what *you'd* call it — whatever psychological-medical jargon you people use — but she was not conscious at the time. That's why she's innocent. She honestly doesn't remember. She'd lost a lot of blood, she'd passed out by the time I'd found her . . .

DOCTOR. You want me to believe that she killed that baby, hid the wastepaper basket, and crawled to the door, all in some sort of mystical trance?

MOTHER. I don't care *what* you believe. You're her psychiatrist, not her jury. You're not determining her guilt.

DOCTOR. Was there ever any question of that?

MOTHER. What do you mean?

DOCTOR. Could someone else have murdered that child? (*silence*)

MOTHER. Not in the eyes of the police.

DOCTOR. And in your eyes?

MOTHER. I've told you what I believe.

DOCTOR. That she was unconscious at the time, yes, so someone else could have easily come into her room and . . . (done it.)

MOTHER. You don't honestly think . . . (something like that happened.)

DOCTOR. It's *possible,* isn't it?

MOTHER. Who?

DOCTOR. I don't know, perhaps one of the other nuns. She found out about the baby and wanted to avoid a scandal.

MOTHER. That's absurd.

DOCTOR. That possibility never occurred to you?

MOTHER. *No one* knew about Agnes' pregnancy. *No one.* Not even Agnes. (*silence*)

DOCTOR. When did you first learn about this innocence of hers, about the way she thinks?

MOTHER. A short while after she came to us.

DOCTOR. And you weren't shocked?

MOTHER. I was appalled. Just as you are now. You'll get used to it.

DOCTOR. What happened?

MOTHER. She stopped eating. Completely.

DOCTOR. This was before her pregnancy?

MOTHER. Almost two years before.

DOCTOR. How long did this go on?

MOTHER. I don't know. I think it was about two weeks before it was reported to me.

DOCTOR. Why did she do this?

MOTHER. She refused to explain at first. She was brought before me — sounds like a tribunal, doesn't it? — and when we were alone she confessed.

DOCTOR. Well?

MOTHER. She said she'd been commanded by God.

(*AGNES appears. Throughout the scene, one of AGNES' hands is inconspicuously hidden in the folds of her habit.*) He spoke to you Himself?

AGNES. No.

MOTHER. Through someone else?

AGNES. Yes.

MOTHER. Who?

AGNES. I can't say.

MOTHER. Why?

AGNES. She'd punish me.

MOTHER. One of the sisters?

AGNES. No.

MOTHER. Who? (*silence*) Why would she tell you to do this?

AGNES. I don't know.

MOTHER. Why do you think?

AGNES. Because I'm getting fat.

MOTHER. Oh, for Heaven's sake.

AGNES. I am. There's too much flesh on me.

MOTHER. Agnes . . .

AGNES. I'm a blimp.

MOTHER. . . . why does it matter whether you're fat or not?

AGNES. Because.

MOTHER. You needn't worry about being attractive here.

AGNES. I do. I have to be attractive to God.

MOTHER. He loves you as you are.

AGNES. No He doesn't. He hates fat people.

MOTHER. Who told you this?

AGNES. It's a sin to be fat.

MOTHER. Why?

AGNES. Look at all the statues. *They're* thin.

MOTHER. Agnes . . .

AGNES. That's because they're suffering. Suffering is beautiful. I want to be beautiful.

MOTHER. Who tells you these things?

AGNES. Christ said it in the Bible. He said, "Suffer the little children, for of such is the Kingdom of Heaven." I want to suffer like a little child.

MOTHER. That's not what . . . (He meant.)

AGNES. I *am* a little child, but my body keeps getting bigger. I don't want it to get bigger because then I won't be able to fit in. I won't be able to squeeze into Heaven.

MOTHER. Agnes, dear, Heaven is not . . . (a place with bars or windows.)

AGNES. (*cupping her breasts*) I mean look at these. I've got to lose weight.

MOTHER. (*reaching toward AGNES*) Oh my dear child.

AGNES. I'm too fat! Look at this—I'm a blimp! God blew up the *Hindenburg*. He'll blow up me. That's what she said.

MOTHER. Who?

AGNES. Mummy! I'll get bigger and bigger every day and then I'll pop! But if I stay little it won't happen!

MOTHER. Your mother tells you this? (*silence*) Agnes, dear, your mother is dead.

AGNES. But she watches. She listens.

MOTHER. Nonsense. I'm your mother now, and I want you to eat.

AGNES. I'm not hungry.

MOTHER. You have to eat *something,* Agnes.

AGNES. No I don't. The host is enough.

MOTHER. My dear, I don't think a communion wafer has the Recommended Daily Allowance of *anything*.

AGNES. Of God.

MOTHER. Oh yes, of God.

AGNES. What does that word mean? Begod?

MOTHER. Bego*t*. You don't know?

AGNES. That God's my father?

MOTHER. Only spiritually. You don't know what that means? Begot?

AGNES. Be*god*. That's what *she* calls it. But I don't understand it. She says it means when God presents us to our mothers, in bundles of eight pounds six ounces.

MOTHER. Oh my dear.

AGNES. I have to be eight pounds again, Mother.

MOTHER. You'd even drop the six ounces. Come here. (*MOTHER reaches out for an embrace. AGNES avoids the embrace, keeping the one hand concealed in her habit. MOTHER stares at the hidden hand.*) Now what's wrong?

AGNES. I'm being punished.

MOTHER. For what?

AGNES. I don't know.

MOTHER. How? (*AGNES presents a hand wrapped in a bloody handkerchief.*) What happened? (*AGNES removes the handkerchief.*) Oh dear Jesus. Oh dear Jesus.

AGNES. It started this morning, and I can't get it to stop. Why me, Mother? Why me?

DOCTOR. How long did it last?

MOTHER. It was gone by the following morning.

DOCTOR. Did it ever come back?

MOTHER. Not that I know of, no.

DOCTOR. Why didn't you send her to a doctor?

MOTHER. I didn't see the need. She began eating again, and that's . . . (all that seemed important at the time.)

DOCTOR. You thought that's all there was to it? Get

some food down her throat and she's all better?

MOTHER. Of course not. Look, I know what you're thinking. She's an hysteric, pure and simple.

DOCTOR. Not simple, no.

MOTHER. I *saw* it. Clean through the palm of her hand, do you think hysteria did that?

DOCTOR. It's been doing it for centuries—she's not unique, you know. She's just another victim.

MOTHER. Yes, God's victim. *That's* her innocence. She belongs to God.

DOCTOR. And I mean to take her away from Him— that's what you fear, isn't it?

MOTHER. You bet I do.

DOCTOR. Well, I prefer to look upon it as opening her mind.

MOTHER. To the world?

DOCTOR. To herself. So she can begin to heal.

MOTHER. But that's not your job, is it? You're here to diagnose, not to heal.

DOCTOR. That is a matter of opinion.

MOTHER. The judge's . . . (opinion.)

DOCTOR. *Your* opinion. I'm here to help her in whatever way I see fit. That's my duty as a doctor.

MOTHER. But not as an employee of the court. You're to make a decision on her sanity as quickly as possible and not interfere with due process of law. Those are the judge's words, not mine.

DOCTOR. As quickly as *I see fit,* not as possible. I haven't made that decision yet.

MOTHER. But the kindest thing you can do for Agnes is to make that decision and let her go.

DOCTOR. Back to court?

MOTHER. Yes.

DOCTOR. And what then? If I say she's crazy, she goes

to an institution. If I say she's sane, she goes to prison.

MOTHER. *Temporary* insanity, then.

DOCTOR. Oh yes. In all good conscience I can say that a child who sees bleeding women at the age of ten, and eleven years later strangles a baby is *temporarily* insane. No, Sister, this case is a little more complicated than that.

MOTHER. But the longer you take to make a decision, the more difficult it will be for Agnes.

DOCTOR. Why?

MOTHER. Because the world is a very damaging experience for someone who hasn't seen it for twenty-one years.

DOCTOR. And you think the sooner she's in prison the better off she'll be?

MOTHER. I'm hoping that whatever her sentence, the judge will allow her to return to the convent and serve her time in penance there. (*silence*)

DOCTOR. Well, we'll see about that.

MOTHER. You wouldn't allow her to return . . . (to the convent?)

DOCTOR. I wouldn't send her back to the source of her problem, no.

MOTHER. *Your* decision has nothing to do with *where* Agnes will serve . . . (her sentence.)

DOCTOR. My *recommendation* has *everything* to do with *everything*.

MOTHER. Then you'd send her to prison?

DOCTOR. Yes, if I felt she was guilty of a premeditated crime, I would.

MOTHER. Or an asylum?

DOCTOR. If I felt it would help her.

MOTHER. It would *kill* her.

DOCTOR. I doubt that.

MOTHER. I'm fighting for this woman's *life*, not her temporal innocence.

DOCTOR. Were you fighting for her life when you didn't even send her to a medical doctor?

MOTHER. What?

DOCTOR. She had a hole in the palm of her hand! She could have bled to death! And you wouldn't send her to a hospital! That child could have died, all because of some stupid . . . (irrational idea that she was better off at the convent.)

MOTHER. But she didn't die, did she?! (*silence*) If anyone else had seen what I had seen, well, she'd be public property. Newspapers, psychiatrists, ridicule. She doesn't deserve that.

DOCTOR. But she has it now.

MOTHER. Yes. She does.

(*AGNES is heard singing. This continues into the next scene.*)

AGNES. *Credo in unum Deum,*
Patrem omnipotentem,
factorem coeli et terrae
visibilium omnium et invisibilium.
Et in unum Dominum Jesum Christum,
Filium Dei unigenitum.
Et ex Patre natum
ante omnia saecula.
Deum de Deo,
lumen de lumine,
Deum verum de Deo vero.
Genitum, non factum,
consubstantialem Patri:
per quem omnia facta sunt.

Qui propter nos homines,
et descendit de coelis.
Et incarnatus est de Spiritu Sancto
ex Maria Virgine:
Et Homo Factus Est.

ACT ONE

Scene 6

AGNES' singing continues through the beginning of
the scene.

DOCTOR. Oh, we would get into terrible arguments, my mother and I. Once, when I was twelve or thirteen, I told her that God was a moronic fairy tale — I think I'd spent an entire night putting those words together — and she said, "How dare you talk that way to me," as if *she* were the slandered party. And shortly after Marie died, I became engaged for a very short time to a very romantic Frenchman whom my mother despised, and whom consequently I adored. We screamed ourselves hoarse many a night over that man. (*She laughs.*) And you know, I haven't thought of him in years. I haven't seen him since I left him — no, *pardonnez-moi,* Maurice, since *he* left me. What finally happened was that I . . . well, I . . . I was pregnant and I didn't exactly see myself as a . . . well, as my mother. Maurice *did,* so . . . (*silence*) And then once, in Mama's last years when she was not altogether lucid, I told her in a burst of anger that God was dead, and do you know what she did? She got down on her knees and prayed for His soul. God love her. I wish we atheists had a set of words that meant as much as those three do. Oh, I was never a devout Catholic—my doubts about the faith began when I was six—but when Marie died I walked away from religion as fast as my mind would take me. Mama never forgave me. And I never forgave the Church. But I learned to live with my anger, forget it even . . . until *she* walked into my office, and every time I saw her after that first lovely moment, I became more and more . . . entranced. (*silence*) Marie. Marie.

ACT ONE

Scene 7

Agnes. Yes, Doctor?

Doctor. Agnes, I want you to tell me how you feel about babies.

Agnes. Oh, I don't like them. They frighten me. I'm afraid I'll drop them. They're always growing, you know. I'm afraid they'll grow too fast and wriggle right out of my arms. They have a soft spot on their heads and if you drop them so they land on their heads they become stupid. That's where I was dropped. You see, I don't understand things.

Doctor. Like what?

Agnes. Numbers. I don't understand where they're all headed. You could spend your whole life counting and never reach the end.

Doctor. I don't understand them either. Do you think I was dropped on my head?

Agnes. Oh, I hope not. It's a terrible thing, one of the great tragedies of life, to be dropped on your head. And there are other things, not just numbers.

Doctor. What things?

AGNES. Everything, sometimes. I wake up and I just can't get hold of the world. It won't stand still.

DOCTOR. So what do you do?

AGNES. I talk to God. *He* doesn't frighten me.

DOCTOR. Is that why you're a nun?

AGNES. I suppose so. I couldn't live without Him.

DOCTOR. But don't you think God works through other religions, and other ways of life?

AGNES. I don't know.

DOCTOR. Couldn't I talk to Him?

AGNES. You could try. I don't know if He'd listen to *you.*

DOCTOR. Why not?

AGNES. Because you don't listen to Him.

DOCTOR. Agnes, have you ever thought of leaving the convent? For something else?

AGNES. Oh no. There's nothing else. It makes me happy. Just being here helps me sleep at night.

DOCTOR. You have trouble sleeping?

AGNES. I get headaches. Mummy did too. She'd lie in the dark with a wet cloth over her face and tell me to go away. Oh, but she wasn't stupid. Oh no, she was very smart. She knew everything. She even knew things nobody else knew.

DOCTOR. What things?

AGNES. The future. She knew what was going to happen to me, and that's why she hid me away. I didn't mind that. I didn't like school very much. And I liked being with Mummy. She'd tell me all kinds of things. She told me I would enter the convent, and I did. She even knew about this.

DOCTOR. This?

AGNES. This.

DOCTOR. Me?

AGNES. This.

DOCTOR. How did she know . . . about this?

AGNES. Somebody told her.

DOCTOR. Who?

AGNES. I don't know.

DOCTOR. Agnes.

AGNES. You'll laugh.

DOCTOR. I promise I won't laugh. Who told her?

AGNES. An angel. When she was having one of her headaches. Before I was born.

DOCTOR. Did your mother see angels often?

AGNES. No. Only when she had her headaches. And not even then, sometimes.

DOCTOR. Do you see angels?

AGNES. (*a little too quickly*) No.

DOCTOR. Do you believe that your mother really saw them?

AGNES. No. But I could never tell her that.

DOCTOR. Why not?

AGNES. She'd get angry. She'd punish me.

DOCTOR. How would she punish you?

AGNES. She'd . . . punish me.

DOCTOR. Did you love your mother?

AGNES. Oh, yes. Yes.

DOCTOR. Did you ever want to become a mother yourself?

AGNES. I could never be a mother.

DOCTOR. Why not?

AGNES. I don't think I'm old enough. Besides, I don't want a baby.

DOCTOR. Why not?

AGNES. Because I don't want one.

DOCTOR. But if you did want one, how would you go about getting one?

AGNES. I'd adopt it.

DOCTOR. Where would the adopted baby come from?

AGNES. From an agency.

DOCTOR. Before the agency.

AGNES. From someone who didn't want a baby.

DOCTOR. Like you?

AGNES. No! Not like me.

DOCTOR. But how would that person get the baby if they didn't want it?

AGNES. A mistake.

DOCTOR. How did your mother get you?

AGNES. A mistake! It was a mistake!

DOCTOR. Is that what she said?

AGNES. You're trying to get me to say that she was a bad woman, and that she hated me, and she didn't want me, but that is not true, because she did love me, and she was a good woman, a saint, and she *did* want me. You don't want to hear the nice parts about her — all you're interested in is sickness!

DOCTOR. Agnes, I cannot imagine that you know nothing about sex . . .

AGNES. I can't help it if I'm stupid.

DOCTOR. . . . that you have no idea who the father of your child was . . .

AGNES. They made it up!

DOCTOR. . . . that you have no remembrance of your impregnation . . .

AGNES. It's not my fault!

DOCTOR. . . . and that you don't believe that you carried a child!

AGNES. It was a mistake!

DOCTOR. What, the child?

AGNES. Everything! Nuns don't have children!

DOCTOR. Agnes . . .

AGNES. Don't touch me like that! Don't touch me like

that! (*AGNES lashes out at the doctor, who moves away.*) I know what you want from me! You want to take God away. You should be ashamed! They should lock *you* up. People like you!

ACT ONE

SCENE 8

MOTHER. You hate us, don't you?

DOCTOR. What?

MOTHER. Nuns. You hate nuns.

DOCTOR. I don't . . . (understand what you're talking about.)

MOTHER. Catholicism, then.

DOCTOR. I hate ignorance and stupidity.

MOTHER. And the Catholic Church.

DOCTOR. I haven't said . . . (anything about the Catholic Church.)

MOTHER. This is a human being you're dealing with, not an institution.

DOCTOR. But . . . (the institution has a hell of a lot to do with the human being.)

MOTHER. Catholicism is not on trial here. I want you to treat Agnes *without* any religious prejudices or turn this case over . . . (to another psychiatrist.)

DOCTOR. (*exploding*) How dare you march into my office and tell me how to run my affairs—

MOTHER. It's my affair too.

DOCTOR. (*overlapping*) . . . how dare you think that I'm in a position to be badgered . . .

MOTHER. I'm only requesting that . . . (you be fair.)

DOCTOR. (*overlapping*) . . . or bullied or whatever

you're trying to do. Who the hell do you think you are? You walk in here expecting applause for the way you've treated this child.

MOTHER. She's not a child.

DOCTOR. And she has a right to *know!* That there is a world out there filled with people who don't believe in God and who are not any worse off than you! People who go through their entire lives without bending their knees once — *to anybody!* And people who still fall in love, and make babies, and occasionally are very happy. She has a right to know that. But you, and your order, and your Church, have kept her ignorant . . .

MOTHER. We could hardly do that . . . (even if we wanted to.)

DOCTOR. . . . because ignorance is next to virginity, right? Poverty, chastity, and ignorance, that's what you live by.

MOTHER. I am not a virgin, Doctor. I was married for twenty-three years. Two daughters. I even have grand-children. Surprised? (*silence*) It might please you to know that I was a failure as a wife and mother. Possibly because I protected my children from *nothing*. Out of the womb and into the "big bad world." They won't see me anymore. That's their revenge. They're both devout atheists. I think they tell their friends I've passed on. Oh don't tell me, Doctor Freud, I'm making up for past mistakes.

DOCTOR. You can help her.

MOTHER. I am.

DOCTOR. No, you're shielding her. *Let* her face the big bad world.

MOTHER. Meaning you.

DOCTOR. Yes, if that's what you think.

MOTHER. What good would it do? No matter what

you decide, it's either the prison or the nuthouse, and the differences between them are pretty thin.

DOCTOR. There's another choice.

MOTHER. What's that?

DOCTOR. Acquittal.

MOTHER. How?

DOCTOR. Innocence. Legal innocence. I'm sure the judge would be happy for *any* reason to throw this case out of court. (*silence*)

MOTHER. What do you want?

DOCTOR. Answers.

MOTHER. Ask.

DOCTOR. When would Sister Agnes have conceived the child?

MOTHER. About a year ago.

DOCTOR. You don't remember anything unusual happening at the convent around that time?

MOTHER. Earthquakes?

DOCTOR. Visitors.

MOTHER. Nothing. She was singing a lot more then, but — oh, dear God.

DOCTOR. What is it?

MOTHER. The sheets.

DOCTOR. What about the sheets?

MOTHER. I should have known, dear God, I should have suspected something.

DOCTOR. What do you mean?

MOTHER. Her sheets. Her sheets had disappeared. One of the sisters complained to me about it. So I called her in. (*AGNES appears.*) Sister Margaret says you've been sleeping on a bare mattress, Sister. Is that true?

AGNES. Yes, Mother.

MOTHER. Why?

AGNES. In medieval days nuns and monks would sleep in their coffins.

MOTHER. We're not in the Middle Ages, Sister.

AGNES. It made them holy.

MOTHER. It made them uncomfortable. If they didn't sleep well, I'm certain the next day they were cranky as mules.

AGNES. Yes, Mother.

MOTHER. Sister, where are your sheets? (*silence*) Do you really believe sleeping on a bare mattress is the equivalent of sleeping in a coffin?

AGNES. No.

MOTHER. Then tell me. Where are your sheets?

AGNES. I burned them.

MOTHER. Why?

AGNES. They were stained.

MOTHER. Sister, how many times have *I* burned into your thick skull and all the other thick skulls of your fellow novices that menstruation is a perfectly natural process and nothing to be ashamed of?

AGNES. Yes, Mother.

MOTHER. Say it.

AGNES. It is a perfectly natural process and nothing to be ashamed of.

MOTHER. Mean it.

AGNES. It is a perfectly . . . (*AGNES begins to cry.*)

MOTHER. A few years ago one of our sisters came to me, in tears, asking for comfort. Comfort because she was too old to have children. Not that she intended to, but once a month she had been reminded of the possibility of Motherhood. So dry your eyes, Sister, and thank God that He has filled you with that possibility.

AGNES. It's not that. It's not that.

MOTHER. What do you mean?

AGNES. It's not my time of the month.

MOTHER. Should you see a doctor?

AGNES. I don't know. I don't know what happened,

Mother. I woke up and there was blood on the sheets, but I don't understand what happened. I don't know what I did wrong. I don't know why I should be punished.

MOTHER. For what?

AGNES. I don't know!

MOTHER. Sister?

AGNES. I don't know! I don't know!

MOTHER. Agnes?

AGNES. I don't know.

MOTHER. Sing something, will you? With me? What's your favorite? "Virgin Mary had one Son . . ."

AGNES. I don't . . .

MOTHER.
"Oh, oh, pretty little baby,
Oh, oh, oh, pretty little baby . . ."

AGNES. I don't know.

MOTHER.
"Glory be to the new-born King."

AGNES. I don't know.

MOTHER.
"Some call Him Jesus,
I think I'll call Him Savior . . ."

MOTHER AND AGNES.
"Oh, oh, I think I'll call Him Savior,
Oh, oh, oh, I think I'll call Him Savior,
Glory be to the new-born King."

AGNES. (*continuing under the next lines*)
"Virgin Mary had one Son,
Oh, oh, pretty little baby,
Oh, oh, oh, pretty little baby,
Glory be to the new-born King."

MOTHER. I sent her to her room. She was calm by then. Said it was nothing. Wouldn't see a doctor. But I should have known.

DOCTOR. Known what?

MOTHER. That was the beginning. That was the night it happened. That is why she burned the sheets.

DOCTOR. What else do you remember about that night?

MOTHER. I'm not certain what night it was.

DOCTOR. Can you find out?

MOTHER. I keep a daybook at the convent.

DOCTOR. And can you check on any unusual activity around that time? You know, earthquakes and visitors?

MOTHER. I'll look in my daybook.

ACT ONE

SCENE 9

DOCTOR. A psychiatrist and a nun died and went to heaven. At the pearly gates, Saint Peter asked them to fill out an application, which they did. Upon looking at their papers, he said, "I see you both were born on the same day in the same year." "Yes," said the doctor. "And that you have the same parents." "Yes," said the nun. "And so you're sisters." The nun smiled knowingly but it was the doctor who answered, "Yes." "And you must be twins," said the saint. "Oh, no," the two of them said, "we're not twins." "Same birthday, same parents, sisters, but not twins?" "Yes," they answered, and smiled. I found this riddle, casually and coincidently, on page 33 of an ancient issue of a defunct magazine. By this time, I was convinced that Agnes was completely innocent. I had begun to believe that someone else had murdered her child. Who that person was, and how I was to prove it, were riddles of my *own* making that I alone could solve. But the only answer I could

come up with was upside down on page 117. (*silence*)
They were two of a set of triplets. My problem was
twofold: I wanted to free Agnes—legally prove her innocence—and I wanted to make her well.

AGNES. I'm not sick!

ACT ONE

SCENE 10

DOCTOR. But you're troubled, aren't you?

AGNES. That's because you keep reminding me. If you
go away, then I'll forget.

DOCTOR. And you're unhappy.

AGNES. Everybody's unhappy! You're unhappy,
aren't you?

DOCTOR. Agnes.

AGNES. Aren't you?

DOCTOR. Sometimes, yes.

AGNES. Only you think you're lucky because you
didn't have a mother who said things to you and did
things that maybe weren't always nice, but that's what
you think, because you don't know that my mother was
a wonderful person, and even if you did know that you
wouldn't believe it because you think she was bad, don't
you.

DOCTOR. Agnes.

AGNES. Answer me! You never answer me!

DOCTOR. Yes, I do think your mother was wrong,
sometimes.

AGNES. But that was because of me! Because *I* was
bad, not her!

DOCTOR. What did you do?

AGNES. I'm always bad.

DOCTOR. What do you do?

AGNES. (*in tears*) No!

DOCTOR. What do you do?

AGNES. I breathe!

DOCTOR. What did your mother do to you? (*AGNES shakes her head.*) If you can't tell me, shake your head, yes or no. Did she hit you? (*"No."*) Did she make you do something you didn't want to do? (*"Yes."*) Did it make you uncomfortable to do this? (*"Yes."*) Did it embarrass you? (*"Yes."*) Did it hurt you? (*"Yes."*) What did she make you do?

AGNES. No.

DOCTOR. You can tell me.

AGNES. I can't.

DOCTOR. She's dead, isn't she?

AGNES. Yes.

DOCTOR. She can't hurt you anymore.

AGNES. She can.

DOCTOR. How?

AGNES. She watches, she listens.

DOCTOR. Agnes, I don't believe that. Tell me. I'll protect you from her.

AGNES. She . . .

DOCTOR. Yes?

AGNES. She . . . makes me . . . take off my clothes and then . . .

DOCTOR. Yes?

AGNES. . . . she makes . . . fun of me.

DOCTOR. She tells you you're ugly?

AGNES. Yes.

DOCTOR. And that you're stupid.

AGNES. Yes.

DOCTOR. And you're a mistake.

AGNES. She says . . . my whole body . . . is a mistake.

DOCTOR. Why?

AGNES. Because she says . . . if I don't watch out . . . I'll have a baby.

DOCTOR. How does she know that?

AGNES. Her headaches.

DOCTOR. Oh yes.

AGNES. And then . . . she touches me.

DOCTOR. Where?

AGNES. Down there. (*silence*) With her cigarette. (*silence*) Please, Mummy. Don't touch me like that. I'll be good. I won't be your bad baby anymore. (*Silence. The DOCTOR puts out her cigarette.*)

DOCTOR. Agnes, dear, I want you to do something. I want you to pretend that I'm your mother. I know that your mother's dead, and you're grown up now, but I want you to pretend for a moment that your mother has come back and that I'm your mother. Only this time, I want you to tell me what you're feeling. All right?

AGNES. I'm afraid.

DOCTOR. (*She takes AGNES' face in her hands.*) Please. I want to help you. Let me help you. (*silence*)

AGNES. All right.

DOCTOR. Agnes, you're ugly. What do you say to that?

AGNES. I don't know.

DOCTOR. Of course you do. Agnes, you're ugly. (*silence*) What do you say?

AGNES. No, I'm not.

DOCTOR. Are you pretty?

AGNES. Yes.

DOCTOR. Agnes, you're stupid.

AGNES. No, I'm not.

DOCTOR. Are you intelligent?

AGNES. Yes, I am.

DOCTOR. Agnes, you're a mistake.

AGNES. I'm not a mistake! I'm here, aren't I? How can I be a mistake if I'm really here? God doesn't make mistakes. *You're* a mistake! I wish you were dead! (*silence*)

DOCTOR. It's all right. Just pretend, right? (*AGNES nods.*) Thank you. (*AGNES begins to cry. The DOCTOR takes her in her arms.*) Agnes, I'd like to ask a favor of you. You can say no, if you don't like what I'm asking.

AGNES. What?

DOCTOR. I'd like permision to hypnotize you.

AGNES. Why?

DOCTOR. Because there are some things that you might be able to tell me under hypnosis that you aren't able to tell me now.

AGNES. Does Mother Miriam know about this?

DOCTOR. Mother Miriam loves you very much just as I love you very much. I'm certain that she wouldn't object . . . (to anything that would help you.)

AGNES. Do you really love me? Or are you just saying that?

DOCTOR. I really love you.

AGNES. As much as Mother Miriam loves me? (*silence*)

DOCTOR. As much as God loves you. (*silence*)

AGNES. All right.

DOCTOR. Thank you. (*DOCTOR embraces AGNES. MOTHER enters, and watches them in silence.*)

MOTHER. I brought the daybook.

DOCTOR. Agnes, you can go now. (*AGNES rises, bows before MOTHER for her blessing, exits. Lighting a cigarette.*) What did you find?

MOTHER. What did *you* find?

DOCTOR. Some facts about her mother.

MOTHER. She wasn't exactly the healthiest of women, was she? Of course I can't speak for her *mental* health, but physically . . .

DOCTOR. You knew her? get out cigarette

MOTHER. We corresponded before her death.

DOCTOR. How old was Agnes when her mother died?

MOTHER. Seventeen.

DOCTOR. Why was she sent to you?

MOTHER. Her mother requested . . . (she be sent to us.)

DOCTOR. Why wasn't she sent to next of kin?

MOTHER. She was. Agnes' mother was my younger sister. (*silence*)

DOCTOR. You lied to me.

MOTHER. About what?

DOCTOR. You said you never saw Agnes until she set foot in the convent.

MOTHER. I didn't. I was a good deal older than my sister. In fact, I was already married before she was born. She was the proverbial black sheep. She ran away from home at an early age. We lost touch with her. When my husband died and I entered the convent, she started writing to me again. She told me about Agnes, and asked me to watch over her in case anything happened.

DOCTOR. And Agnes' father?

MOTHER. Could have been any one of a dozen men, from what my sister told me. She was afraid that Agnes would follow in her footsteps. She did everything to prevent that.

DOCTOR. By keeping her home from school.

MOTHER. Yes.

DOCTOR. And listening to angels.

MOTHER. She drank too much. That's what killed her.

DOCTOR. Do you know what she did to Agnes?

MOTHER. I don't think I . . . (care to know.)

DOCTOR. She molested her. (*silence*)

MOTHER. Oh dear Jesus.

DOCTOR. There *is* more here than meets the eye, isn't there? *Lots* of dirty little secrets. Pull back the sheets and what do you find? A niece.

MOTHER. I didn't tell you because I didn't think it was important.

DOCTOR. No, it just makes you doubly responsible, doesn't it? Blood runs thicker, right?

MOTHER. Had I known what Agnes was suffering . . .

DOCTOR. Why didn't you?! My God, you knew she was keeping the child from school. You knew she was an alcoholic.

MOTHER. I knew that *after* . . . (the fact.)

DOCTOR. Why didn't you do anything to stop her?!

MOTHER. I didn't know! And that's no answer, is it? (*silence*)

DOCTOR. What did you find in the daybook?

MOTHER. Agnes was sick the Sunday before she told me about the sheets. If she burned them then, they probably became stained on Saturday night. Unfortunately, on that night one of our elder nuns passed away. I have no recollection of any visitors to the convent. I was needed in the sickroom.

DOCTOR. Was Extreme Unction given on that night?

MOTHER. Yes, of course.

DOCTOR. So Father Marshall would have been present.

MOTHER. Yes, but you can't believe . . . (that Father Marshall could have done it.)

DOCTOR. Somebody has to be responsible for that child. If it wasn't Father Marshall, who else could it be? (*silence*) Well, we'll find out soon enough. I've gotten Agnes' permission to hypnotize her.

MOTHER. And *my* permission?

DOCTOR. I don't think you have anything to say in this matter.

MOTHER. I'm her guardian.

DOCTOR. She's twenty-one years old; she doesn't need a guardian.

MOTHER. But she must come to me first and ask permission.

DOCTOR. Does this mean you'll deny it?

MOTHER. I haven't decided that yet.

DOCTOR. This woman's health is at stake.

MOTHER. Her spiritual health.

DOCTOR. I don't give a good goddamn about what you call . . . (her spiritual health.)

MOTHER. I know you don't.

DOCTOR. Sentence her and be done with it, that's what you're saying. Well, *I* can't . . . (do that yet.)

MOTHER. What I'm saying is that you have a beautifully simple woman . . .

DOCTOR. An unhappy woman.

MOTHER. But she was happy with us. And she could go on being happy if she were left alone.

DOCTOR. Then why did you call the police in the first place? Why didn't you throw the baby in the incinerator and be done with it?

MOTHER. Because I'm a moral person, that's why.

DOCTOR. Bullshit!

MOTHER. Bullshit yourself!

DOCTOR. The Catholic Church doesn't have a corner on morality, Mother.

MOTHER. Who said anything about the Catholic Church?

DOCTOR. You just said . . . (that you . . .)

MOTHER. What the hell does the Catholic Church have to do with you?

DOCTOR. Nothing. Absolutely nothing.

MOTHER. What have we done to hurt you?

DOCTOR. (*beginning to speak*) (Nothing.)

MOTHER. And don't deny it. Oh, I can smell an ex-Catholic a mile away. What did we do? Burn a few heretics? Sell some indulgences? But those were in the days when the Church was a ruling body. We let governments do those things today.

DOCTOR. Just because you don't have the power you once had . . .

MOTHER. Oh, I'm not interested in the Church as power, Doctor. I'm interested in it as simplicity and peace. I know, it's very difficult to find that in *any* institution nowadays. So tell me. What did we do to you? You wanted to neck in the back seat of a car when you were fifteen and you couldn't because it was a sin. So instead of questioning that one little rule—

DOCTOR. It wasn't sex. It was a lot of things, but it wasn't sex. It started in the first grade when my best friend was run over by a cement truck on her way to school. The nun said she died because she hadn't said her morning prayers.

MOTHER. Stupid woman.

DOCTOR. Yeah.

MOTHER. That's all?

DOCTOR. That's all?! That's enough. She was a *beautiful* little girl . . . (and to explain away her death like that . . .)

MOTHER. What has that got to do with it?

DOCTOR. I wasn't! She was the pretty one, and she died. Why not me? I hadn't said my morning prayers either. And I was ugly. Not just plain. Ugly! I was fat,* I had big buck teeth, ears out to here, and freckles all over my face. Sister Mary Cletus used to call me Polka-Dot Livingstone. (*The DOCTOR is laughing in spite of herself.*)

MOTHER. So you left the Church because you had freckles?

DOCTOR. No, because . . . Yeah, I left the Church because I had freckles. And guess what?

MOTHER. What?

DOCTOR. (*smiling*) That's also why I hate nuns.

(*AGNES is heard singing, then humming until indicated.*)

AGNES. *Sanctus, sanctus, sanctus,*
Dominus Deus Sabaoth.
Pleni sunt coeli et terra gloria tua.

Hosanna in excelsis.
Benedictus qui venit in nomine Domini.
Hosanna in excelsis.

DOCTOR. Why is that so important to you, her singing?

MOTHER. When I was a child I used to speak with my guardian angel. Oh, I don't ask you to believe that I heard loud, miraculous voices, but just as some children have invisible playmates, I had angelic conversations. Like Agnes' mother, you might say, but I was a lot younger then, and I am not Agnes' mother. Anyway, when I was six I stopped listening and my angel stopped

*or scrawny

speaking. But just as a sailor remembers the sea, I remembered that voice. I grew, fell in love, married and was widowed, joined the convent, and shortly after I was chosen Mother Superior, I looked at myself one day and saw nothing but a survivor of an unhappy marriage, a mother of two angry daughters, and a nun who was certain of nothing. Not even of Heaven, Doctor Livingstone. Not even of God. And then one evening, while walking in a field beside the convent wall, I heard a voice and looking up I saw one of our new postulants standing in her window, singing. It was Agnes, and she was beautiful; and all of my doubts about God and myself vanished in that one moment. I recognized the voice. (*silence*) Don't take it away from me again, Doctor Livingstone. Those years after six were very bleak.

DOCTOR. My sister died in a convent. And it's *her* voice *I* hear. (*AGNES stops singing. Silence.*) Does my smoking still bother you?

MOTHER. No, it only reminds me.

DOCTOR. Would you like one?

MOTHER. I would love one, but no thank you.

DOCTOR. Once, years ago at the beginning of "the scare," I decided to stop. I had no idea how many cigarettes I smoked then, but I used a book of matches a day. So I came up with the ingenious plan of cutting back on matches. First a half book, then a quarter of a book, then down to three or four a day. And look at what happened. I can't even eat without a cigarette in my hand. I can't go to weddings or funerals, plays, concerts. But some days I can go fourteen hours on a single match. Remarkable, isn't it? Do you think the saints would have smoked, had tobacco been popular?

MOTHER. Undoubtedly. Not the ascetics, of course, but, well, Saint Thomas More . . .

DOCTOR. Parliaments.

MOTHER. Saint Ignatius, I think, would smoke Camels and then stub them out on the soles of his feet. Of course all the Apostles—

DOCTOR. Hand-rolled.

MOTHER. Yes, and even Christ would partake socially.

DOCTOR. Saint Peter, the original Marlboro man.

MOTHER. Mary Magdalene?

DOCTOR. You've come a long way, baby.

MOTHER. Saint Joan would chew Mail Pouch.

DOCTOR. (*taking a toke*) And what, do you suppose, are today's saints smoking?

MOTHER. There are no saints today. Good people, yes. But extraordinarily good people? I'm afraid those we are sorely lacking.

DOCTOR. Do you believe they ever existed, these extraordinarily good people?

MOTHER. Yes, I do.

DOCTOR. Would you like to become one?

MOTHER. To become? One is born a saint. Only no one is born a saint today. We've evolved too far. We're too complicated.

DOCTOR. But you can try, can't you? To be good?

MOTHER. Oh yes, but goodness has very little to do with it. Not all the saints were good. In fact, most of them were a little crazy. But their hearts were with God, left in His hands at birth. "Trailing clouds of glory." No more. We're born, we live, we die. Occasionally one might appear among us, still attached to God. But we cut that cord very quickly. No freaks here. We're all solid, sensible men and women, feet on the ground, money in the bank, innocence trampled underfoot. Our minds dissected, our bodies cut open, "No soul here; must have been a delusion." We look at the sky, "No

God up there, no heaven, no hell." Well, we're better off. Less disease, for one thing. No *room* for miracles. But oh my dear, how I miss the miracles.

DOCTOR. Do you really believe miracles happened?

MOTHER. Of course I do. I believe in the miracle of the loaves and fishes two thousand years ago as strongly as I would doubt it today. What we've gained in logic we've lost in faith. We no longer have any sort of . . . primitive wonder. The closest we come to a miracle today is in bed. And we give up everything for it. Including those bits of light that might still, by the smallest chance, be clinging to our souls, reaching back to God.

DOCTOR. The saints had lovers.

MOTHER. Oh yes, the saints had lovers, but then the cord was a rope. Now it's a thread.

DOCTOR. Do you believe Agnes is still attached to God?

MOTHER. Listen to her singing.

DOCTOR. Time to begin.

MOTHER. Begin what?

DOCTOR. The hypnotism. You still disapprove?

MOTHER. Will it stop you if I do?

DOCTOR. No.

MOTHER. May I be present?

DOCTOR. Yes. Of course.

MOTHER. Then let's begin.

(*Blackout*)
INTERMISSION

ACT TWO

Scene 1

AGNES. (*singing*) *Basiez moy, ma doulce amye,*
Par amour je vous en prie
Non feray. Et pour quoy?
Se je faisoie la folie,
Ma mère en seroit morrie.
Velâ de quoy, velâ de quoy.

DOCTOR. The hypnosis took weeks to achieve, not minutes. An hour a day, spaced in between a kleptomaniac and an exhibitionist. Between lunch and dinner. Between Phil Donahue and Dan Rather. Between sleepless nights. Endless weekends. But *my* memories, oh, *they* come *too* easily. Sometimes they won't even let me finish a sentence. They come galloping out, mid-thought. I know if only I could finish the thought, they would . . . (go away.)

ACT TWO

Scene 2

AGNES. I'm frightened!

DOCTOR. Don't be. I cannot make you say or do anything you do not wish to say or do. Sit back and relax. Fine. Now imagine that you are listening to a chorus of angels. Their music is so beautiful and so real that you can touch it. It surrounds you like a very warm and comfortable pool of water. The water is so warm you hardly know that it's there. All of the muscles in your body are melting into the pool. The water is just under your chin. But you must remember that this water is music, and if you are submersed in it you can still breathe freely and deeply. Now the water covers your chin. Your mouth, your nose, and your eyes. Close your eyes, Agnes. Thank you. When I count to three, you will wake up. Can you hear me?

AGNES. Yes.

DOCTOR. Who am I?

AGNES. Doctor Livingstone.

DOCTOR. And why am I here?

AGNES. To help me.

DOCTOR. Good. Would you like to tell me why you're here?

AGNES. Because I'm in trouble.

DOCTOR. What kind of trouble? (*silence*) What kind of trouble, Agnes?

AGNES. I'm frightened.

DOCTOR. Of what?

AGNES. Of telling you.

DOCTOR. But it's easy. It's only a breath with sound. Say it. What kind of trouble, Agnes?

(*AGNES struggles, then says:*)

AGNES. I had a baby. (*silence*)

DOCTOR. How did you have a baby?

AGNES. It came out of me.

DOCTOR. Did you know it was going to come out?

AGNES. Yes.

DOCTOR. Did you want it to come out?

AGNES. No.

DOCTOR. Why?

AGNES. Because I was afraid.

DOCTOR. Why were you afraid?

AGNES. Because I wasn't worthy.

DOCTOR. To be a mother?

AGNES. Yes.

DOCTOR. Why?

(*AGNES begins to cry softly.*)

AGNES. May I open my eyes now?

DOCTOR. Not yet. Very soon, but not yet. Do you know how the baby got into you?

AGNES. It grew.

DOCTOR. What made it grow? Do you know?

AGNES. Yes.

DOCTOR. Would you like to tell me?

AGNES. No.

DOCTOR. Did you know from the beginning that you were going to have a baby?

AGNES. Yes.

DOCTOR. How did you know?

AGNES. I just knew.

DOCTOR. What did you do about it?

AGNES. I drank lots of milk.

DOCTOR. Why?

AGNES. Because that's good for babies.

DOCTOR. You wanted the baby to be healthy?

AGNES. Yes.

DOCTOR. Then why didn't you go to a doctor?

AGNES. Nobody would believe me.

DOCTOR. That you were having a baby?

AGNES. No, not that.

DOCTOR. What wouldn't they believe? (*silence*) Agnes, did anyone else know about the baby?

AGNES. Yes.

DOCTOR. Who?

AGNES. I don't want to tell you.

DOCTOR. Did you tell this other person or did this other person guess?

AGNES. She guessed.

DOCTOR. One of your fellow sisters.

AGNES. Yes.

DOCTOR. Will she be angry if you tell me her name?

AGNES. She made me promise not to.

DOCTOR. All right, Agnes, I'm going to ask you to open your eyes in a moment. When you do, you will see your room at the convent. It is the night about four months ago when you were very sick. Around six o'clock in the evening.

AGNES. I'm afraid.

DOCTOR. Don't be. I'm here. All right?

AGNES. Yes.

DOCTOR. Now tell me what you did this evening before you went to bed.

AGNES. I ate.

DOCTOR. What did you have for dinner?

AGNES. Fish. Brussels sprouts.

DOCTOR. You don't like brussels sprouts?

AGNES. I hate them.

DOCTOR. What else?

AGNES. A little coffee. Some sherbet for dessert. That was special.

DOCTOR. And then what?

AGNES. We got up, cleared the table, and went to chapel for vespers.

DOCTOR. Yes?

AGNES. I left early because I wasn't feeling very well.

DOCTOR. What was wrong?

AGNES. Just tired. I had my milk . . . (and went to bed.)

DOCTOR. Who gave you your milk?

AGNES. Sister Margaret, I think.

DOCTOR. Was it Sister Margaret who knew about the baby? (*silence*) All right, Agnes, let's go to your room. Ready?

AGNES. Yes.

DOCTOR. I want you to open your eyes, and to see your room as you saw it on that night. What do you see?

AGNES. My bed.

DOCTOR. What else is in the room?

AGNES. A chair.

DOCTOR. Where is that?

AGNES. Here.

DOCTOR. Anything else?

AGNES. A crucifix.

DOCTOR. Above the bed?

AGNES. Yes.

DOCTOR. Anything else? (*silence*) Agnes? What do you see? Something different?

AGNES. Yes.

DOCTOR. Something that's not normally in the room?

AGNES. Yes.

DOCTOR. What is that?

AGNES. A wastepaper basket. (*silence*)

DOCTOR. Do you know who put it there?

AGNES. No.

DOCTOR. Why do you think it's there?

AGNES. For me to get sick in.

DOCTOR. Are you ill?

AGNES. Yes.

DOCTOR. What do you feel?

AGNES. A pain in my stomach. I feel as if I've eaten glass. (*She holds her stomach in a contraction.*)

DOCTOR. What do you do?

AGNES. I have to throw up. (*She tries.*) I can't. (*contraction*) It's glass! One of the sisters has fed me glass!

DOCTOR. Which one?

AGNES. I don't know which one. They're all jealous, that's why.

DOCTOR. Of what?

AGNES. Of me! (*contraction*) Oh God. Oh my God. Water. It's all water!

DOCTOR. Why doesn't anyone come?

AGNES. They can't hear me.

DOCTOR. Why not?

AGNES. They're all in vespers.

DOCTOR. Can you get them?

AGNES. I can't. It's clear on the other side of the building. (*contraction*) Oh no, please. Please. I don't want this to happen. I don't want it.

DOCTOR. Where are you?

AGNES. On the bed. (*contraction*) Oh God. Oh my God. (*sharp intake of breath*)

DOCTOR. What is it?

AGNES. Get away from me.

DOCTOR. Who?

AGNES. Go away! I don't want you here!

DOCTOR. Is someone in the room with you? Agnes?

AGNES. Don't touch me! Don't touch me! Please! Please don't touch me! (*contraction*) No, I don't want to have the baby now. I don't want it! Why are you making me do this? . (*Contraction. She begins to scream.*)

DOCTOR. It's all right, Agnes. No one's going to hurt you.

AGNES. You want to hurt my baby! You want to take my baby! (*contraction*)

MOTHER. Stop her, she'll hurt herself!

DOCTOR. No, let her go . . . (for a moment.)

MOTHER. (*rushing to AGNES*) I'm not going on with this . . . (anymore.)

DOCTOR. No!

(*As MOTHER touches her, AGNES screams, striking MOTHER and pushing her away.*)

AGNES. You're trying to take my baby! You're trying to take my baby! (*scream and contraction*) Stay in! Please stay in! (*several violent and final contractions*)

MOTHER. Stop her! Help her!

AGNES. BITCH! It's not my fault, Mummy. WHORE! It's a mistake, Mummy. LIAR!

DOCTOR. Agnes, it's all right. One, two, three. It's all right. (*AGNES relaxes.*) It's me. Doctor Livingstone. It's all right. Thank you. Thank you. How do you feel?

AGNES. Frightened.

DOCTOR. It's hard enough to go through it once, isn't it?

AGNES. Yes.

DOCTOR. Do you remember what just happened?

AGNES. Yes.

DOCTOR. Good. Do you think you're well enough to stand?

AGNES. Yes. (*She does.*)

DOCTOR. There.

(*AGNES embraces the DOCTOR. As she leaves, she begins to sing.*)

AGNES. *Ave Maria,*
Gratia plena,
Dominus tecum.

Benedicta tu in mulieribus,
Et benedictus fructus ventris tui, Jesu.

MOTHER. You've formed your opinion about her, haven't you?

DOCTOR. She's a very disturbed young woman, but . . . (I don't feel that's all there is to it.)

MOTHER. Your job is done.

DOCTOR. As far as the court is concerned, yes, but personally—

MOTHER. Personally?! I don't think you were asked to become personally involved.

DOCTOR. But I am.

MOTHER. And I'm asking you to get the hell out! If we want to hire a psychiatrist for Agnes, we'll find our own, thank you.

DOCTOR. One who'll ask her the questions you want asked.

MOTHER. One who will approach this matter with some objectivity and respect!

DOCTOR. For you?!

MOTHER. For Agnes.

DOCTOR. You still believe that my interference will destroy some sort of . . . (special aura about her?)

MOTHER. She's a remarkable person, Doctor.

DOCTOR. That doesn't make her a saint.

MOTHER. I never said she was.

DOCTOR. But that's what you believe, isn't it?

MOTHER. That she's been touched by God, yes.

DOCTOR. Prove that to me! She sings—is that unique? She hallucinates, stops eating, and bleeds spontaneously. Is that supposed to convince me that she shouldn't be touched? I want a miracle! Nothing less. *Then* I'll leave her be. (*silence*)

MOTHER. The father.

DOCTOR. Who is he?

MOTHER. Why must he be anybody?

DOCTOR. (*laughing*) You're as crazy as the rest of your family.

MOTHER. I don't know if it's true, I . . . (only think it might be possible.)

DOCTOR. How?

MOTHER. I don't . . . (know.)

DOCTOR. Do you think a big white dove came flying through her window?

MOTHER. No, I can't believe that.

DOCTOR. That would be a little scary, wouldn't it? Second Coming Stopped by Hysterical Nun.

MOTHER. This is *not* the Second Coming, Doctor Livingstone. Don't misunderstand me.

DOCTOR. But you just said . . . (there isn't any father.)

MOTHER. If this is true—and I mean *if*—it's nothing more than a slightly miraculous *scientific* event.

DOCTOR. Nothing more? Oh come on, Mother, you don't expect me to believe garbage . . . (like that.)

MOTHER. You can believe what you like. I only told you because . . . (you asked for a miracle.)

DOCTOR. If this is some miracle of science, there must be a reasonable explanation.

MOTHER. But a miracle is an event *without* an explanation. That's why people like you fail to believe, because you demand an explanation, and when you don't get one you create one.

DOCTOR. What the hell are you talking about?

MOTHER. Unanswered questions. Tiny discrepancies in what people like you say is the way of the world.

DOCTOR. This is insane.

MOTHER. The mind is a remarkable thing, Doctor Livingstone. You know that as well as I do. People bend spoons, stop watches. Zen archers split arrows down the center, one after another. We haven't *begun* to explore the mind's possibilities. If she's capable of putting a hole in her hand without benefit of a nail, why couldn't she split a tiny cell in her womb?

DOCTOR. Hysterical parthenogenesis, is that what you mean?

MOTHER. Partheno what?

DOCTOR. The female's ability in lower life forms to reproduce alone.

MOTHER. I don't pretend to . . . (understand it biologically.)

DOCTOR. If frogs can do it, why not Agnes.

MOTHER. Two thousand years ago, some people believe, a man was born without a father. Now no intelligent person today accepts that without question. We want answers, yes, that's the nature of science, but look at the answers we provide. An angel came to the woman in a shaft of light, hysterical parthenogenesis. If those are the answers, the answers are crazy. If those are the answers, no wonder people like you don't believe in miracles.

DOCTOR. The virgin birth was a lie told to a cuckolded husband by a frightened wife.

MOTHER. Oh, *that's* a plausible explanation. That's what you're looking for, right? Plausibility! But I believe that it is also the nature of science to wonder, and we can only wonder if we are willing to question *without* finding all the answers.

DOCTOR. But we *can* find them.

MOTHER. You can *look* for them. There's a difference. There was *no* man at the convent on that night, and there was *no* way for any man to get in or out.

DOCTOR. So you're saying God did it.

MOTHER. No! That's as much as saying Father Marshall did it. I'm saying God permitted it.

DOCTOR. But how did it happen?

MOTHER. You'll never find the answer to everything, Doctor. One and one is two, yes, but that leads to four and then to eight and soon to infinity. The wonder of science is not in the answers it provides but in the questions it uncovers. For every miracle it finally explains, ten thousand more miracles come into being.

DOCTOR. I thought you didn't believe in miracles today?

MOTHER. But I *want* to believe. I want the *opportunity* to believe. I want the *choice* to believe.

DOCTOR. What you are choosing to believe is a lie. Because you don't want to face the fact that she was raped, or seduced, or that *she* did the seducing.

MOTHER. She is an innocent.

DOCTOR. But she's not an enigma. Everything that Agnes has done is explainable by modern psychiatry. She's an hysteric. She was molested as a child. She had no father, an alcoholic mother. She was locked in a house until she was seventeen and in a convent until she was twenty-one. One-two-three, right down the line.

MOTHER. Is that what you believe, that she's the sum of her psychological parts?

DOCTOR. That's what I *have* to believe.

MOTHER. Then why are you so obsessed with her? (*silence*) You're losing sleep, thinking of her all the time, bent on saving her. Why? That's a question, no answer needed. I'm not accusing, I'm recognizing. The symptoms are very familiar. *I* know. I'm an expert on the disease. We're in this together, you and I. (*silence*)

DOCTOR. So you believe that God permitted her . . .

MOTHER. Possibly.

DOCTOR. Possibly permitted her to have a child . . .

MOTHER. Not divine.

DOCTOR. Not divine, just a child, without benefit of man.

MOTHER. That's what I would like to believe, yes.

DOCTOR. Without proof?

MOTHER. Definitely without proof. There's no infallible proof for virginity. Only an absence of proof against it.

DOCTOR. Then how do you explain the bloody sheets on the night of the conception?

MOTHER. I can't.

DOCTOR. And why did the baby die?

MOTHER. I don't . . . (know.)

DOCTOR. Do you think God made a mistake and tried to correct it?

MOTHER. Don't be . . . (absurd.)

DOCTOR. Or is this all a hoax, a cover-up, to lead me down the garden path?

MOTHER. Why would I want to do that?

DOCTOR. Because this is murder we're talking about.

MOTHER. Murder?

DOCTOR. You believe Agnes is innocent. Well, I believe she's innocent too — of this crime. Like you, I have no proof. But I'm looking, and if it's there, I'll find it.

MOTHER. Don't try to turn this into some kind of murder mystery, Doctor.

DOCTOR. Aren't you concerned about what she just told us? About that other person in the room?

MOTHER. I'm concerned about her . . . (health and her safety.)

DOCTOR. Who *was* that other person, Mother? Was it you?!

MOTHER. If you persist in believing that this is a case

of murder, then it is the district attorney you must consult, not me. And definitely not Agnes. (*MOTHER turns to leave.*)

DOCTOR. Where are you going?

MOTHER. To the court. To have you taken off this case.

DOCTOR. Why? Am I getting too close . . . (to the truth?)

MOTHER. Doctor, I pray that—

DOCTOR. Agnes is innocent, isn't she?

MOTHER. (*overlapping*)—someday you may understand my position.

DOCTOR. *Isn't she?*

MOTHER. Good-bye, Doctor. Oh, and as for that miracle you wanted, it *has* happened. It's a very small one, but you'll notice it soon enough. (*MOTHER leaves. AGNES enters.*)

AGNES. You were fighting.

DOCTOR. (*quickly and secretly*) Agnes, listen. You must help me. Has Mother Miriam ever threatened you in any way?

AGNES. No.

DOCTOR. Or frightened you?

AGNES. Why are you asking that?

DOCTOR. Because I believe she . . . (may have something to do with—)

MOTHER. (*offstage*) Sister Agnes!

AGNES. Coming, Mother!

DOCTOR. Agnes, who . . . (was in the room with you?)

AGNES. I won't see you again, will I?

DOCTOR. Yes, you will. I promise. Agnes, who was in the room with you? (*silence*) Do you know?

AGNES. Yes.

DOCTOR. Who was it? For the love of God, tell me.

AGNES. It was my mother.
MOTHER. (*offstage*) Agnes!
AGNES. Good-bye. (*AGNES leaves.*)

ACT TWO

SCENE 3

DOCTOR. I dreamt that night that I was a midwife in a small private hospital in a faraway land. I was dressed in white and the room I was in was white, and a window was open and I could see mountains of snow all around. Below me on a table lay a woman prepared for a cesarean. She began to scream and I knew I had to cut the baby out as quickly as possible. I slipped a knife into her belly, then reached to my wrists inside. Suddenly I felt a tiny hand grab hold of my finger and begin to pull, and the woman's hands pressed down on my head, and the little creature inside drew me in, to the elbows, to the shoulders, to the chin, but when I opened my mouth to scream—I woke up, to find my sheets spotted. With blood. *My* blood. My rather sporadic menstrual cycle had ceased altogether some three years before, but on that night it began again. (*silence*) What would I have done with a child? Nothing. Nothing. (*silence*) The next day I asked for and received an order from the court allowing Agnes to return to my care. You see, I was so sure I was right. As a doctor, perhaps, I should have known better, but as a person—(*She begins to beat her chest with her fist.*) I am not made of granite. I am made of flesh and blood . . . and heart . . . and soul. . . . (*She continues viciously to beat her chest in silence for a few moments, then stops.*) This is it. The unfinished thought. The last reel. No alternate in sight.

ACT TWO

SCENE 4

MOTHER. Well, you've won, haven't you?

DOCTOR. Not at all, not yet.

MOTHER. You've decided to take . . . (her apart.)

DOCTOR. I've decided to hypnotize her again.

MOTHER. Hasn't she had enough?

DOCTOR. And I want to ask you a few questions that I wasn't able to ask you before . . .

MOTHER. I'm all ears.

DOCTOR. . . . because you very cleverly steered away from them.

MOTHER. My God, but you're vindictive.

DOCTOR. You're hiding something from me and I want to know the truth.

MOTHER. Then ask.

DOCTOR. Did Agnes ever say anything to you about not feeling well, while she was carrying the child?

MOTHER. Yes, she did.

DOCTOR. Then why didn't you send her to a doctor?

MOTHER. She wouldn't go.

DOCTOR. Wouldn't she?

MOTHER. No, she was afraid.

DOCTOR. Of what? That he might find something out? Is that what she told you? Or did you guess that?

MOTHER. If you're going to continue to persecute me . . . (I'll stop this conversation immediately.)

DOCTOR. I'm not persecuting you; I'm asking you a question.

MOTHER. I'm a nun, and you hate . . . (nuns.)

DOCTOR. Did you know that she was pregnant?!

(Silence. MOTHER desperately tries to fight back and hide her tears. Then she speaks.)

MOTHER. Yes.

DOCTOR. And you didn't send her to a doctor?

MOTHER. It was too late.

DOCTOR. What do you mean?

MOTHER. I didn't guess it until — *(Silence. MOTHER fights for control.)*

DOCTOR. Until when? Don't waste those tears on me, Mother. Until when?

MOTHER. Until it was too late.

DOCTOR. For what? An abortion?

MOTHER. Don't be absurd.

DOCTOR. Too late for what?!

MOTHER. I don't know, too late to stop it!

DOCTOR. The baby?

MOTHER. The scandal! It was too late to stop it but I had to try. I had to keep it quiet. I made her promise not to tell anyone. I had to have time to think.

DOCTOR. And you didn't get it, did you?

MOTHER. No! That night when she was ill, I knew . . .

DOCTOR. That time had run out?

MOTHER. Yes.

DOCTOR. So you went to her room to help her with the birth.

MOTHER. She didn't want help.

DOCTOR. But *you* wanted the child out of the way as quickly as possible.

MOTHER. That's a lie.

DOCTOR. You hid the wastepaper basket in the room.

MOTHER. I didn't hide it! I put it there for the blood and the dirty sheets . . .

DOCTOR. And the baby.

MOTHER. No!

DOCTOR. You tied the cord around its neck . . .

MOTHER. I simply wanted her to have it when no one was around. I would have taken the baby to a hospital and left it with them. But there was so much blood, I panicked.

DOCTOR. Before or after you killed the child?

MOTHER. I left it with her! I went for help!

DOCTOR. I doubt that's what she'll say.

MOTHER. Then she's a goddamn liar! (*MOTHER covers her face with her hands. AGNES is heard singing.*)

AGNES. *Agnus Dei,*
qui tollis peccata mundi,
miserere nobis.
Agnus Dei,
qui tollis peccata mundi,
miserere nobis.
Agnus Dei,
qui tollis peccata mundi,
dona nobis pacem.

MOTHER. All right. Let's finish this once and for all. (*MOTHER exits. She gently takes AGNES' face between her hands. Alone, the DOCTOR begins to cross herself, but stops. AGNES enters, followed by MOTHER.*)

DOCTOR. Hello, Agnes.

AGNES. Hello.

DOCTOR. I have some more questions I'd like to ask you. Is that all right?

AGNES. Yes.

DOCTOR. And I would like to hypnotize you again. Is that all right too?

AGNES. Yes.

DOCTOR. Good. Sit down. Relax. You're going to enter the pool of water again. Only this time, I want you to imagine that there are holes in your body, and the warm water is flowing into those holes, behind your eyes, warm, so warm, so clean, like prayer, your eyes are so heavy, so . . . sleepy. Close your eyes. When I count to three, you'll wake up. Agnes, can you hear me?

AGNES. Yes.

DOCTOR. Who am I?

AGNES. Doctor Livingstone.

DOCTOR. And who is with me?

AGNES. Mother Miriam Ruth.

DOCTOR. Fine. Now Agnes, I'm going to ask you a few questions, and I'd like you to keep your eyes closed. All right?

AGNES. Yes.

DOCTOR. I would like you to remember, if you can, one night about a year ago, a Saturday night, when one of the sisters in the convent died.

MOTHER. Sister Paul.

DOCTOR. The night when Sister Paul died. Do you remember?

AGNES. Yes.

DOCTOR. What's the matter?

AGNES. I liked Sister Paul.

DOCTOR. Agnes, what happened that night?

AGNES. She sent me to bed early.

DOCTOR. Who did?

AGNES. Mother.

DOCTOR. Did you go to bed?

AGNES. Yes.

DOCTOR. Imagine that you are in your room, Agnes. Tell us what happened.

AGNES. I woke up.

DOCTOR. What time is it?

AGNES. I don't know. It's still dark.

DOCTOR. Do you see anything?

AGNES. Not at first. But . . .

DOCTOR. What?

AGNES. Someone is in the room.

DOCTOR. Are you frightened?

AGNES. Yes.

DOCTOR. What do you do? (*silence*) Agnes?

AGNES. Who is it? (*silence*) Who's there? (*silence*) Is it you? (*silence*) But I *am* afraid. (*silence*) Yes. (*silence*) Yes I do. (*silence*) Why me? (*silence*) Wait. I want to see you! (*She gasps and opens her eyes.*)

DOCTOR. What do you see?

AGNES. A flower. Waxy and white. A drop of blood, sinking into the petal, flowing through the veins. A tiny halo. Millions of halos, dividing and dividing, feathers are stars, falling, falling into the iris of God's eye. Oh my God, he sees me. Oh, it's so lovely, so blue, yellow, green leaves brown blood, no, red, His Blood, my God, my God, I'm bleeding, I'M BLEEDING! (*She is bleeding from the palms of her hands.*)

MOTHER. Oh my God.

AGNES. I have to wash this off, it's on my hands, my legs, my God, it's on the sheets, help me clean the sheets, help me, help me, it won't come out, the blood won't come out!

MOTHER. (*grabbing her*) Agnes . . .

AGNES. Let go of me!

MOTHER. Agnes, please . . .

AGNES. You wanted this to happen, didn't you?! You prayed for this to happen, didn't you?!

MOTHER. No, I didn't.

AGNES. Get away from me! I don't want you any-more! I wish you were dead!

DOCTOR. Agnes . . .

AGNES. I wish you were all dead!

DOCTOR. . . . we had nothing to do with that man in your room.

AGNES. Let me alone!

DOCTOR. Do you understand? He did a very bad thing to you.

AGNES. Don't touch me!

DOCTOR. He frightened you, and he hurt you.

AGNES. Don't!

DOCTOR. It's not your fault . . .

AGNES. Mummy!

DOCTOR. . . . it's his fault.

AGNES. Mummy's fault!

DOCTOR. Tell us who he is so we can find him . . .

AGNES. (*to MOTHER*) Your fault!

DOCTOR. . . . and stop him from doing this to other women.

AGNES. (*to MOTHER*) It's all your fault!

DOCTOR. Agnes, who did you see in the room?!

AGNES. I hate him.

DOCTOR. Of course you do. Who was he?

AGNES. I hate him for what he did to me.

DOCTOR. Yes.

AGNES. For what he made me go through.

DOCTOR. Who?

AGNES. I hate him!

DOCTOR. Who did this to you?

AGNES. God! God did it to me! It was God! And now I'll burn in hell because I hate Him!

DOCTOR. Agnes, you won't burn in hell. It's all right to hate him.

MOTHER. That's enough for today, wake her up.

DOCTOR. Not yet.

MOTHER. She's tired and she's not well, and *I'm* taking her home.

DOCTOR. She doesn't belong to you anymore.

MOTHER. She belongs to God.

DOCTOR. She belongs to *me,* and she's staying here!

MOTHER. You can't . . . (keep her here.)

DOCTOR. Agnes, what happened to the baby?

MOTHER. She can't remember!

DOCTOR. Yes she can! Agnes . . .

MOTHER. She doesn't remember!

DOCTOR. (*grabbing AGNES*) . . . what happened to the baby?!

AGNES. They threw it away.

DOCTOR. No, after the birth.

AGNES. It was dead.

MOTHER. Don't do this to her!

DOCTOR. It was alive, wasn't it?

AGNES. I don't remember.

MOTHER. Please!

DOCTOR. It was alive, wasn't it?

MOTHER. Don't do this to *me!*

DOCTOR. *Wasn't it?*

AGNES. YES!!! (*silence*)

DOCTOR. What happened?

AGNES. I don't want to remember.

DOCTOR. But you do, don't you?

AGNES. Yes.

DOCTOR. Mother Miriam was with you, wasn't she?

AGNES. Yes.

DOCTOR. She took the baby in her arms . . .

AGNES. Yes.

DOCTOR. You saw it all, didn't you?

AGNES. Yes.

DOCTOR. And then . . . what did she do? (*silence*) Agnes, what did she do?

AGNES. (*simply and quietly*) She left me alone with that little . . . thing. I looked at it and thought, this is a mistake. But it's my mistake, not Mummy's. God's mistake. I thought, I can save her. I can give her back to God. (*silence*)

DOCTOR. What did you do?

AGNES. I put her to sleep.

DOCTOR. How?

AGNES. I tied the cord around her neck, wrapped her in the bloody sheets, and stuffed her in the trash can.

MOTHER. No. (*MOTHER turns away. Silence.*)

DOCTOR. One. Two. Three. (*AGNES slowly rises and walks away, humming "Charlie's Neat" softly to herself.*) Mother? (*silence*) Mother, please . . .

(*MOTHER turns to face the doctor.*)

MOTHER. You were right. She remembered. And all this time I thought she was some unconscious innocent. Thank you, Doctor Livingstone. We need people like you to destroy all those lies that ignorant folk like myself pretend to believe.

DOCTOR. Mother . . .

MOTHER. But I'll never forgive you for what you've taken away. (*silence*) You should have died. Not your sister. You.

AGNES. (*speaking to an unseen friend*) Why are you crying? (*The DOCTOR and the MOTHER turn to her. Silence.*) But *I* believe. I *do*. (*silence*) Please, don't you leave me too. Oh no. Oh my God, O sweet Lady, don't leave me. Please, please don't leave me. I'll be good. I won't be your bad baby anymore. (*She sees someone else.*) No, Mummy. I don't want to go with you. Stop pulling me. Your hands are hot. Don't touch me like that! Oh my God, Mummy, don't burn me! DON'T BURN ME! (*Silence. She turns to MOTHER and the*

*DOCTOR and stretches out her hands like a statue of
the Lady, showing her bleeding palms. She smiles, and
speaks simply and sanely.*) I stood in the window of my
room every night for a week. And one night I heard the
most beautiful voice imaginable. It came from the middle of the wheat field beyond my room, and when I
looked I saw the moon shining down on Him. For six
nights He sang to me. Songs I'd never heard. And on the
seventh night He came to my room and opened His
wings and lay on top of me. And all the while He sang.
(*Smiling and crying, she sings.*)
"Charlie's neat and Charlie's sweet,
And Charlie he's a dandy,
Every time he goes to town,
He gets his girl some candy.
Over the river and through the trees,
Over the river to Charlie's,
Over the river and through the trees,
To bake a cake for Charlie.
(*MOTHER begins to take AGNES off.*)
"Charlie's neat and Charlie's sweet,
And Charlie he's a dandy,
Every time he goes to town,
He gets his girl some candy.
Oh, he gets his girl some candy."

ACT TWO

Scene 5

DOCTOR. (*singing*) "Yes, he gets his girl some candy."
I don't know the truth behind that song. Yes, perhaps it
was a song of seduction, and the father was . . . a field

hand. Or perhaps the song was simply a remembered lullaby sung many years before. And the father was . . . hope, and love, and desire, and a belief in miracles. (*silence*) I never saw them again. The following day I removed myself from the case. Mother Miriam threw Agnes on the mercy of the court, and she was sent to a hospital . . . where she stopped singing . . . and eating . . . and where she died. Why? Why was a child molested, and a baby killed, and a mind destroyed? Was it to the simple end that not two hours ago this doubting, menstruating, non-smoking psychiatrist made her confession? What kind of God can permit such a wonder one as her to come trampling through this well-ordered existence?! I want a reason! I *want* to believe that she was . . . blessed! And I *do* miss her. And I hope that she has left something, some little part of herself, with *me*. That would be miracle enough. (*silence*) Wouldn't it?

PROP LIST

2 Chairs — 1 arm chair, 1 straight-back chair
1 Ashtray — Free-standing, office-type, with handle
1 Pack cigarettes, opened
1 Cigarette lighter
1 handkerchief with stigmata effect
blood effect

COSTUME PLOT

1 Psychiatrist suit
1 Mother Superior outfit
1 Postulate outfit

TALKING WITH . . .

(LITTLE THEATRE)

By JANE MARTIN

11 women—Bare stage

Here, at last, is the collection of eleven extraordinary monologues for eleven actresses which had them on their feet cheering at the famed Actors Theatre of Louisville—audiences, critics and, yes, even jaded theatre professionals. The mysteriously pseudonymous Jane Martin is truly a "find", a new writer with a wonderfully idiosyncratic style, whose characters alternately amuse, move and frighten us always, however, speaking to us from the depths of their souls. The characters include a baton twirler who has found God through twirling; a fundamentalist snake handler, an ex-rodeo rider crowded out of the life she has cherished by men in 3-piece suits who want her to dress up "like Minnie damn Mouse in a tutu"; an actress willing to go to any length to get a job; and an old woman who claims she once saw a man with "cerebral walrus" walk into a McDonald's and be healed by a Big Mac. "Eleven female monologues, of which half a dozen verge on brilliance."—London Guardian. "Whoever (Jane Martin) is, she's a writer with an original imagination."—Village Voice. "With Jane Martin, the monologue has taken on a new poetic form, intensive in its method and revelatory in its impact."—Philadelphia Inquirer. "A dramatist with an original voice . . . (these are) tales about enthusiasms that become obsessions, eccentric confessionals that levitate with religious symbolism and gladsome humor."—N.Y. Times. *Talking With* . . . is the 1982 winner of the American Theatre Critics Association Award for Best Regional Play. (#22009)

HAROLD AND MAUDE

(ADVANCED GROUPS—COMEDY)

By COLIN HIGGINS

9 men, 8 women—Various settings

Yes: *the Harold and Maude!* This is a stage adaptation of the wonderful movie about the suicidal 19 year-old boy who finally learns how to truly *live* when he meets up with that delightfully whacky octogenarian, Maude. Harold is the proverbial Poor Little Rich Kid. His alienation has caused him to attempt suicide several times, though these attempts are more cries for attention than actual attempts. His peculiar attachment to Maude, whom he meets at a funeral (a mutual passion), is what saves him—and what captivates us. This new stage version, a hit in France directed by the internationally-renowned Jean-Louis Barrault, will certainly delight both afficionados of the film and new-comers to the story. "Offbeat upbeat comedy."—Christian Science Monitor. (#10032)

Other Publications for Your Interest

A WEEKEND NEAR MADISON
(LITTLE THEATRE—COMIC DRAMA)
By KATHLEEN TOLAN

2 men, 3 women—Interior

This recent hit from the famed Actors Theatre of Louisville, a terrific ensemble play about male-female relationships in the 80's, was praised by *Newsweek* as "warm, vital, glowing . . . full of wise ironies and unsentimental hopes". The story concerns a weekend reunion of old college friends now in their early thirties. The occasion is the visit of Vanessa, the queen bee of the group, who is now the leader of a lesbian/feminist rock band. Vanessa arrives at the home of an old friend who is now a psychiatrist hand in hand with her naif-like lover, who also plays in the band. Also on hand are the psychiatrist's wife, a novelist suffering from writer's block; and his brother, who was once Vanessa's lover and who still loves her. In the course of the weekend, Vanessa reveals that she and her lover desperately want to have a child—and she tries to persuade her former male lover to father it, not understanding that he might have some feelings about the whole thing. *Time Magazine* heard "the unmistakable cry of an infant hit . . . Playwright Tolan's work radiates promise and achievement." (#25051)

PASTORALE
(LITTLE THEATRE—COMEDY)
By DEBORAH EISENBERG

3 men, 4 women—Interior
(plus 1 or 2 bit parts and 3 optional extras)

"Deborah Eisenberg is one of the freshest and funniest voices in some seasons."—Newsweek. Somewhere out in the country Melanie has rented a house and in the living room she, her friend Rachel who came for a weekend but forgets to leave, and their school friend Steve (all in their mid-20s) spend nearly a year meandering through a mental landscape including such concerns as phobias, friendship, work, sex, slovenliness and epistemology. Other people happen by: Steve's young girlfriend Celia, the virtuous and annoying Edie, a man who Melanie has picked up in a bar, and a couple who appear during an intense conversation and observe the sofa is on fire. The lives of the three friends inevitably proceed and eventually draw them, the better prepared perhaps by their months on the sofa, in separate directions. "The most original, funniest new comic voice to be heard in New York theater since Beth Henley's 'Crimes of the Heart.'"—N.Y. Times. "A very funny, stylish comedy."—The New Yorker. "Wacky charm and wayward wit."—New York Magazine. "Delightful."—N.Y. Post. "Uproarious . . . the play is a world unto itself, and it spins."—N.Y. Sunday Times. (#18016)

Other Publications for Your Interest

THE CURATE SHAKESPEARE AS YOU LIKE IT
(LITTLE THEATRE—COMEDY)
By DON NIGRO

4 men, 3 women—Bare stage

This extremely unusual and original piece is subtitled: "The record of one company's attempt to perform the play by William Shakespeare". When the very prolific Mr. Nigro was asked by a professional theatre company to adapt *As You Like It* so that it could be performed by a company of seven he, of course, came up with a completely original play about a rag-tag group of players comprised of only seven actors led by a dotty old curate who nonetheless must present Shakespeare's play; and the dramatic interest, as well as the comedy, is in their hilarious attempts to impersonate all of Shakespeare's multitude of characters. The play has had numerous productions nationwide, all of which have come about through word of mouth. We are very pleased to make this "underground comic classic" widely available to theatre groups who like their comedy wide open and theatrical.   (#5742)

SEASCAPE WITH SHARKS AND DANCER
(LITTLE THEATRE—DRAMA)
By DON NIGRO

1 man, 1 woman—Interior

This is a fine new play by an author of great talent and promise. We are very glad to be introducing Mr. Nigro's work to a wide audience with *Seascape With Sharks and Dancer*, which comes directly from a sold-out, critically acclaimed production at the world-famous Oregon Shakespeare Festival. The play is set in a beach bungalow. The young man who lives there has pulled a lost young woman from the ocean. Soon, she finds herself trapped in his life and torn between her need to come to rest somewhere and her certainty that all human relationships turn eventually into nightmares. The struggle between his tolerant and gently ironic approach to life and her strategy of suspicion and attack becomes a kind of war about love and creation which neither can afford to lose. In other words, this is quite an offbeat, wonderful love story. We would like to point out that the play also contains a wealth of excellent **monologue** and **scene material.**   (#21060)

Other Publications for Your Interest

HUSBANDRY
(LITTLE THEATRE—DRAMA)

By PATRICK TOVATT

2 men, 2 women—Interior

At its recent world premiere at the famed Actors Theatre of Louisville, this enticing new drama moved an audience of theatre professionals up off their seats and on to their feet to cheer. Mr. Tovatt has given us an insightful drama about what is happening to the small, family farm in America—and what this means for the future of the country. The scene is a farmhouse whose owners are on the verge of losing their farm. They are visited by their son and his wife, who live "only" eight hours' drive away. The son has a good job in the city, and his wife does, too. The son, Harry, is really put on the horns of a dilemma when he realizes that he is his folks' only hope. The old man can't go it alone anymore—and he needs his son. Pulling at him from the other side is his wife, who does not want to leave her job and uproot her family to become a farm wife. *Husbandry*, then, is ultimately about what it means to be a *husband*—both in the farm and in the family sense. *Variety* praised the "delicacy of Tovatt's dialogue", and called the play "a literate exploration of family responsibilities in a mobile society." Said *Time*: "The play simmers so gently for so long, as each potential confrontation is deflected with Chekhovian shrugs and silences, that when it boils into hostility it sears the audience." (#10169)

CLARA'S PLAY
(LITTLE THEATRE—DRAMA)

By JOHN OLIVE

3 men, 1 woman—Exterior

Clara, an aging spinster, lives alone in a remote farmhouse. She is the last surviving member of one of the area's most prominent families. It is summer, 1915. Enter an immigrant, feisty soul named Sverre looking for a few days' work before moving on. But Clara's farm needs more than just a few days' work, and Sverre stays on to help Clara fix up and run the farm. It soon becomes clear unscrupulous local businessmen are bilking Clara out of money and hope to gain control of her property. Sverre agrees to stay on to help Clara keep her family's property. "A story of determination, loyalty. It has more than a measure of love, of resignation, of humor and loyalty."—Chicago Sun-Times. "A playwright of unusual sensitivity in delineating character and exploring human relationships." —Chicago Tribune. "Gracefully-written, with a real sense of place."—Village Voice. A recent success both at Chicago's fine Wisdom Bridge Theatre and at the Great American Play Festival of the world-reknowned Actors Theatre of Louisville; and, on tour, starring Jean Stapleton. (#5076)